Oh, Brother!

Adapted by Sarah Nathan

Based on the series created by Todd J. Greenwald

Part One is based on the episode, "Justin's Little Sister," Written by Eve Weston

Part Two is based on the episode, "Alex in the Middle," Written by Matt Goldman

DISNEP PRESS

New York

PART ONE

Chapter One

Alex Russo sat in Mr. Laritate's social studies class, talking to her best friend, Harper Evans. She kept her eye on the door, waiting for their teacher to walk in. Just as the bell rang, he entered the classroom. He was dressed in his usual suit, but instead of a regular necktie he was wearing a bolo tie, a traditional cowboy neckpiece. "All right, my little history wranglers, enough ruckus!" Mr. Laritate bellowed.

"Let's start off Thursday's class as we always do." He paused and waited for his usual punch line. "With an oral pop quiz!"

All the students groaned. Alex turned to Harper, who was sitting behind her. "Oh, my gosh," she said sarcastically. "It's the Thursday pop quiz we have *every* Thursday. I'm totally caught off guard." She rolled her eyes at her friend.

Mr. Laritate scanned the classroom to see who he would call on first. "In no particular order," he said, "Wendy Bott, you're up! The French and Indian War was fought by three groups of people. Name two of them."

Wendy stood up and fidgeted nervously. "Um . . . the French was one for sure," she stuttered. "And the other one . . . I'm just going to guess, Indians?"

Mr. Laritate grinned. "Excellent!" he exclaimed as he rang the large cowbell sitting on his desk. He called on the next student.

"Nellie Rodriguez, you're up. The War of 1812 started in what year?"

"Oh, my gosh," Nellie said nervously. "I studied for this one." She quickly looked down at her hand where she had written the answer. "Uh . . . 1812?"

Once again, Mr. Laritate rang his bell. "Another winner!" Suddenly, he zoned in on Alex. "Alex Russo," he said. "The Monroe Doctrine. What is it? When was it passed? And please give a two-minute argument defending it."

Alex couldn't believe it. Everyone else had gotten such easy questions! This was totally unfair.

"Hold on," she said as she stood up. "The other two questions had the answers *in* them. My question's supposed to be: the Monroe Doctrine—whose doctrine is it? I'd say 'Monroe' and you'd say, "Yipee-dilly-willy, way-to-go-little-filly.'"

"Oh, Alex," groaned Mr. Laritate, shaking his head disapprovingly. "You are *definitely* not your brother Justin."

"No, I'm not," Alex agreed. "I'm cuter and more fun to talk to. And I don't have dental floss on a key chain."

Mr. Laritate grinned and reached for something in his pocket. "Yeah, well, I do!" he exclaimed, pulling out a key chain that had dental floss hanging from it. "Justin made it for me." Mr. Laritate let out a sigh. "Ah, Justin. Those were the days."

As Alex sat down, she turned back to Harper. "Can you believe this?" she asked. "He's comparing me to Justin!"

"I know. It is so hard to live up to Justin," Harper said sympathetically. Then she got a dreamy look on her face as she thought about him. "He's smart and handsome, and he has the *healthiest* gums. I mean—"

Alex held up her hand. "Okay, I get it! He

flosses. Let's make him president!" She turned back around in her seat and slumped down in her chair. This was going to be a long social studies class!

In the kitchen of the Waverly Sub Station, the restaurant that the Russo family owned and ran, Mrs. Russo put on her apron. She was getting ready to prepare some sandwiches just as Alex and Justin walked in.

"How was school today?" she asked. She looked at Alex and then over at Justin. "Wait, let me guess. Who got in trouble?" she commented, looking directly at her daughter once again. She knew full well that Alex had a tendency to always get into some sort of trouble.

Justin smirked as Alex reached over to open the freezer door. The door actually opened into the Wizard's Lair, the room where Mr. Russo gave Alex and her brothers wizard lessons every Tuesday and Thursday after school. Each of the Russo children had magic powers, and they were all wizards-in-training. Their dad had given up his wizard powers when he married their mom, a nonwizard. Now he gave lessons to his kids so that they would be prepared for the family wizard competition when they turned eighteen. Only one of the Russo kids would win and remain a wizard, so the stakes were seriously high.

Alex sighed and turned back to her mom. "Well, I got a hard quiz question because of Justin, got in trouble because of Justin, and got recruited by the math team because of Justin," she complained. She turned and headed into the lair. Life would be a whole lot easier without Justin around, Alex thought woefully.

Mrs. Russo raised her eyebrows at Justin, who was looking smug. "What are you smiling about?" she asked.

"I have had a much more productive day than I realized," he gloated.

Chapter Two

When Alex walked into the lair, her dad was getting things organized for the day's wizard lesson. Her younger brother, Max, was already seated, waiting for the lesson to start. Justin followed Alex into the room, and Mr. Russo looked at the trio and smiled. "Okay. Today's lesson is about genies," he announced.

Max sighed. "Oh, I know a Jeannie," he said with a dreamy look in his eyes. "Jeannie Kowalski. *Jeannies* do not like it when you flick them in the ear. That's lesson number one."

"No, lesson number one is: leave that girl alone," his dad said. "She's bigger than you. And lesson number two is about genies that live in lamps." He pointed to a drawing of a genie lamp on the blackboard. "They are the con artists of the wizard world," he warned.

"Con artists?" Alex asked. "I thought they were supposed to grant you three wishes."

"They do," Justin commented. "But they take your wish and they twist it around into something you wish you never wished for."

Max perked up. "Is Alex a genie?" he asked.

Mr. Russo and Justin both laughed.

"No," Mr. Russo said. "She's just your older sister. But good, Max. You understand the concept."

"Well, no genie can trick me," Alex said confidently. "I'd make them wish that they never met me."

Justin sat down on the couch. "You don't have to be a genie to wish you never met you," he said arrogantly.

Shooting her brother a look, Alex reached out and grabbed the genie lamp on the table. "So, are we going to take this genie out or what?"

"You can't take the genies out of their lamps, because they're tricky!" Justin exclaimed, jumping up and grabbing the lamp away from Alex. He cradled the lamp in his arms. "Once you get them out, it's hard to get them back in."

"Yeah, Alex," Mr. Russo told her. "This was all in the handout, which you *obviously* didn't read." He took the lamp from Justin and gently placed it back on the table. "Why can't you be more like your brother?"

Alex fell back into her chair. "Because I don't want to grow old alone!" she declared.

"Wait a minute," Max interrupted. He looked

from the genie lamp to his dad. "So we're getting a genie lesson without seeing a genie?"

"No, the genie is not coming out of the lamp," Mr. Russo said. Then he smiled. "We're going into the lamp." He turned around to Justin. "Come on. Justin, take us in."

The four Russos grabbed hands and stood in a circle. Justin closed his eyes. In a deep voice, he chanted, "We're now small and teeny-weeny, take us inside to see the genie."

Suddenly, the four of them were inside the small lantern! It was decorated with gold and red fabrics, with a plush couch in the middle. Just then, a genie wearing a purple and gold outfit appeared.

"Oh, Christmas carolers!" the genie cried. "It's a little early, but who doesn't love a little "Jingle Bell Rock"? Hit it, boys. A one, two, a one, two, three, four—"

Mr. Russo interrupted her. "Uh, hi. We're not carolers. We're on a field trip," he explained. "I'm just showing these young wizards what a genie looks like in its natural habitat."

The genie stopped. "Oh, I'm sorry. I wasn't expecting company. I don't have enough food," she said, looking down at the tray in her hands. It was piled high with treats. She threw the tray over her shoulder to get rid of the evidence. "But I know this amazing pizzeria—everybody likes pizza, right?—on Eighty-sixth and Columbus, with a topping bar."

"A *topping* bar?" Alex asked, moving closer to the genie.

"How's that for a topper?" the genie asked, smiling.

"That sounds great," Alex told her. They grabbed hands. "Let's get out of here!"

The genie beamed. "Oh, let's!" she cried.

"We are now small and teeny-weeny," Alex began to chant. "But instead—"

Justin clapped his hand over his sister's

mouth. He couldn't believe how fast Alex had fallen for the genie's bluff. "See that, Dad?" he asked. "She thought a genie wouldn't outsmart her, and she almost set her free."

"*Hello*," Alex said sarcastically. "I was about to put my hand over my own mouth."

Mr. Russo nodded his head. "This is why I brought you here," he explained. "To show you how tricky genies can be."

"That's right," the genie added with a serious expression. "Genies can be very tricky." Then she turned to Alex with a sly grin on her face. "Hey, let's go talk about it over a latte. There's this place in Brooklyn that makes these lattes with basil in them!"

"Ooh, basil lattes! That sounds great," Alex cooed. "Why don't you get your jacket and we'll go?"

"Yes!" the genie whispered to herself as she rushed off to get her coat.

Alex turned to her father. "See that? I just

outsmarted the genie." She reached to grab hands with her father and brothers. "Now, let's get out of here."

As they joined hands, her dad broke out in a smile. "And I just found out there's a pizzeria with a topping bar," he said. "Take us out!"

"We are now small and teeny-weeny," Justin chanted. "We are done visiting the genie." And with that, the Russos magically transported themselves to the pizzeria.

Chapter Three

The next day, Alex rushed into Mr. Laritate's classroom, hoping to arrive early for once. Luckily, no one was in the room when she got there. Alex pulled the genie's lamp out of her bag. She had snuck it out of the house earlier that morning—she wanted to make a wish just to see what would happen. She took a deep breath and rubbed its side. How cool would it be if Justin disappeared for a while? she thought. Then I wouldn't have to hear about how great he is all the time!

Suddenly, the genie appeared on Mr. Laritate's desk. She was dressed more casually than before, and she was holding a plunger and a live snake!

"Oh, it's you," the genie said when she saw Alex. "I was just in the middle of snaking my drain." She snapped her fingers, and everything in her hands disappeared. She hopped off the desk and stood in front of Alex.

"Okay," she said, sighing. She took a deep breath and began her usual speech. "Thank you for rubbing my lamp. I know you have a lot of choices in lamps, and I appreciate your choosing mine. Your wish is my command. You are entitled to three wishes. Blah, blah, blah. Not valid in Vermont or Connecticut."

This was exactly what Alex had hoped for! "Okay," she said anxiously. "I wish people would stop comparing me to Justin."

"Oh, your older brother?" she asked.

"He seems really sharp. I'm glad he's not my brother. I could never live in that shadow."

"That's what I'm talking about!" Alex exclaimed. "Let's get to the wish."

"Yay!" the genie squealed happily. Suddenly, a scoreboard appeared on the chalkboard with a large *X* under a number one.

"Okay, you're good," the genie said. "You will no longer be compared to your brother." Then she leaned in closer to Alex. "So, you probably heard genies are always trying to sneak off," she said.

"You can't sneak off if I'm letting you go," Alex said simply.

The genie was confused. "You're letting me go?" she asked.

"Sure," Alex said, shrugging. "Go on. I got my wish." She waved the genie away.

The genie snickered as the bell rang for class.

Alex pushed her toward the door. "Class is starting," she said. "Beat it."

"Thank you!" the genie exclaimed, giddy with excitement.

"No, thank *you*," Alex corrected her, and shoved the genie out the door as students started walking into class.

Just then, Mr. Laritate entered the classroom. "Okay, my wily coyotes," he said. "It's time for a surprise Thursday pop quiz on *Friday*." He looked around the room and his eyes landed on Alex. "Alex Russo."

"Here we go," Alex muttered to herself. She hoped that the genie's magic was about to work.

"Name two of the three people who were on the Lewis and Clark expedition, which also featured Sacagawea," Mr. Laritate said.

Alex couldn't believe her ears. "Uh, did you just give me all three answers?" she asked, shocked.

"I'm not giving hints," Mr. Laritate said firmly.

Alex smiled and gave her response. "Okay," she said. "Then I'm going to say Lewis and Clark. *And* Sacagawea."

"Wow!" Mr. Laritate exclaimed. "Three out of three! And I only asked for two. I think we have a winner! Let's let Alex ring the bell!"

Surprised, Alex stared at her teacher. "Is there somebody you want to compare me to?" she asked, expecting to hear at least *something* about Justin.

Mr. Laritate looked confused. "No," he said.

Alex smiled. Then she went up to her teacher's desk and rang the cowbell. "Thank you, genie," she said under her breath. Sweet, she thought. No more being compared to my annoying older brother. This is going to be *awesome*.

Chapter Four

"Can you believe it?" Alex asked Harper as they walked down the hall after class. "Mr. Laritate didn't ask me some ridiculous question that only Justin would know the answer to."

Harper turned to Alex with a confused look on her face. "Who's Justin?" she asked.

"What do you mean, 'Who's Justin?'" Alex asked as she opened her locker. She turned around and saw that her brother had just arrived. "Hey, Justin," she said.

"Alex, the weirdest thing just happened to me," he said nervously. "I got kicked out of chemistry because I wasn't on the class list. And I told Mrs. Rieber it had to be a mistake, I've been there all semester, but she still didn't remember me."

"Oh, that *is* weird," Alex said slowly. Harper hadn't remembered Justin either . . . something was definitely wrong.

"You'd think she'd remember the student who came up with the periodic-element song," Justin continued. He took a breath and sang, "Hydrogen then helium. Lithium, beryllium. Boron . . ."

"Speaking of *bor*ons," Alex snipped, "why don't you go tell your *friends* about your big problem." She motioned to a group of guys down the hall.

"Fine," Justin huffed and walked over to his friends.

Harper leaned in closer to Alex. "*That's*

Justin?" she cooed. "The new guy who's H-O-T cute?"

"No, the guy who's my brother, and who's V-E-R-Y dorky," Alex replied.

Harper gave Alex an odd look. "No, you only have one brother," she stated. "His name is Max."

"Oh. My. Gosh!" Alex shouted as all the pieces fell into place and she realized what had happened. "Harper, I'm going to catch up with you later," she said, running off.

"Fine," Harper called after her. "But I call dibs on that new Justin guy. I liked him first."

"Dibs acknowledged," Alex called back. Justin was down the hall now, talking to one of his friends . . . who didn't seem to remember him, either.

"We played video games together. Yesterday. Remember?" Justin pleaded. "I got overexcited and hyperventilated. Your mom had to get me a bag."

"Sorry, dude," Justin's friend said. "Good luck with whatever." The guy had no clue who Justin was!

Turning to face Alex, Justin looked like he was about to explode. "I don't have any friends. My teacher doesn't remember me. *What did you do?*"

"Why?" Alex cried. "Just because something completely out of the ordinary happens, doesn't mean I automatically had something to do with it."

But Alex's guilty expression told Justin everything. "*Did* you have something to do with it?" he asked, pointing an accusing finger at her.

Alex took a deep breath. "Yes," she admitted sheepishly.

Justin groaned. He looked around the crowded school hallway. How could no one remember him?

"I-I made a wish with the genie that

everyone would stop comparing me to you, but I guess she did that by making everyone *forget* you," Alex blurted out.

Justin took a deep breath. "Okay," he said slowly. Now that he understood the problem, he figured there must be a simple solution. "Well, you tell the genie you wish everyone remembers me again."

"I can't," Alex told him. "I let her go." She flashed Justin a smile. "That way she couldn't sneak off."

"Oh, I get it," Justin said in mock understanding. "It's kind of like giving a burglar your money so he doesn't steal it."

Alex threw up her arms. "Look, what do you want me to do?"

"You've done enough," Justin snapped. "We're going to have to get Dad to help us."

After school, Alex and Justin walked into the Waverly Sub Station. Mr. Russo was busy waiting on tables, but he came over when he saw them walk in. He immediately extended his hand to Justin.

"Hi. I'm Jerry, Alex's father," he said. "Nice to meet you." Then he went off to take an order from a table in the back of the restaurant.

"We already met!" Justin cried, shocked at what his own father had just said.

Alex sighed. "I don't think Dad's going to help us," she mumbled. Then, Mrs. Russo came out of the kitchen. Maybe *she* would remember Justin! Alex thought.

"Hey, who's your new friend?" Mrs. Russo said, pulling Alex aside. She leaned in closer to Alex. "He looks a little like your Uncle Ernesto."

Alex was speechless. Could this get *any* worse?

Meanwhile, the consequences of Alex's wish were becoming clearer to Justin. "It's not just school. *No one* remembers me!" he shouted.

Putting her arm around him, Alex tried to be sympathetic. "Look on the bright side," she said sweetly. "I bet you don't have to do dishes tonight."

But from the look on Justin's face, Alex knew that washing the dishes was the last thing he was worried about!

Chapter Five

Alex grabbed Justin's hand and pulled him into the restaurant kitchen so they could discuss this unfolding disaster in private. She had to make him feel better about his *non*existence, and convince him that she would figure out how to fix her latest magical mess!

"Okay, Justin, I know this looks bad," she said. "No one remembers you. But I'll fix it." She flashed him a big grin. "In the meantime, think of all the benefits!"

Justin glared at his sister. "You mean, like not having to do the dishes?"

"Yeah!" Alex said enthusiastically. Although she realized that this was not a very effective argument, she was trying to stay positive.

Justin turned away. "I'd trade that for my parents remembering me," he mumbled. Then something dawned on him. "Where am I supposed to sleep tonight?" he suddenly cried out.

"I fell asleep at table five one night," Alex said, pointing to a table in the restaurant's dining room. "It's pretty comfortable."

Justin went over to the wall and banged his head against it. This situation was getting worse by the minute!

Now Alex knew she had to spring into action. She took a deep breath, trying to clear her head. "Okay," she said, thinking quickly. "Follow my lead," she commanded as she walked back out into the restaurant.

Rubbing his hand on his sore head, Justin

sighed and followed Alex out of the kitchen. Alex quickly pulled their mother, who was nearby, aside.

"Mom," she said urgently; she had to play this just right. "Justin's parents are out of town for a week, and he doesn't have a place to stay, and he lost his key when he tripped, and it fell down the subway grate," she said, rushing to get the words out.

"Oh, my goodness," Mrs. Russo gasped. She looked over at Justin sympathetically. "Well, Justin, you're more than welcome to stay with us until your parents get back."

"Really?" Justin asked. He was touched by his mother's hospitality.

"Mm-hmm," she said, and then went to take an order from a customer.

"Thank you," Justin called after her.

"See that?" Alex said proudly. "Problem solved."

"Yeah, everything's great," he said. "It's just

my parents don't know who I am!" he cried, throwing his hands up in the air.

Just then, Max Russo walked into the restaurant. Justin had never been so glad to see his little brother! Surely Max would remember him!

"Hey, Max!" he cried out. "Do, uh, you still remember me, buddy?"

"Of course I do," Max said.

"You do?" Justin exclaimed. Finally— someone knew who he was!

"Yes!" Max told him. "You're Uncle Ernesto. I've seen you in Mom's pictures."

Justin's shoulders slumped. This situation was getting worse by the second!

Just then, the door to the Sub Station flew open and Harper rushed in. She was holding a large ceramic sculpture. She ran over to Alex.

"Alex!" Harper said excitedly. "Look what I made in art class!"

Alex looked at what Harper made and

shook her head. It was a sculpture of Justin's head, and it looked just like him!

Harper peered around Alex. "Oh, my gosh!" she cried. "He's here!" She tugged on Alex's arm, getting her complete attention. "How do I look?"

Alex glanced at the artwork Harper was holding. "Better than him!" she laughed, referring to the sculpture. Then she turned to include Justin in their conversation. "Justin," she said, calling him over, "look who's here. And she made something"—Alex paused, searching for just the right word to describe the art—"nice-ish."

"Uh, hey, Harper," Justin said politely.

Harper took a step back in surprise. "You know my name?" She gasped. She held the sculpture out toward Justin. "I made this for you." She blushed when she realized that there were three lipstick marks on the sculpture's face—all shaped like kisses! "Oh, that's not my lipstick on the cheek," she quickly added.

"Thanks, Harper," Justin said as he took the sculpture. "I'll put it in my room." He gave Alex a frustrated look. "As soon as my parents get back in town," he said as he walked away.

"Oh, where are you staying?" Harper called after him.

"Here," Alex answered.

"He's already moved in?" Harper asked with a frown. "You do *not* respect the code of dibs!" she spat out and then turned and stormed out of the restaurant.

Justin walked back over to his sister. "Alex, we have to do something," he urged.

"You know, they can't forget you. You're their firstborn!" Alex said, trying to remain positive. "Maybe we can jog their memory."

Together they walked over to the table that their parents were cleaning off.

Justin paused and then started talking nervously. "Uh, Mr. Russo and Mrs. Russo," he said formally. "Since I'll be staying with you, it would be rude if I didn't let you get to know me."

Mr. Russo smiled. "So, tell us about yourself," he said.

"Uh, well, Justin loves school," Alex offered. She swung her arm around his shoulder.

"*Loves* school?" Mrs. Russo asked enthusiastically. "Oh, we never hear that around here!"

"And I love watching sports with my dad," Justin added. He moved closer to his father and chuckled. "Go, Mets!"

"Ooh, a Mets fan!" Mr. Russo exclaimed. "You should've started with that. Now, Jets or Giants?"

"Jets," Justin said, knowing how much his dad loved the Jets.

Mr. Russo grinned and held out his hand. "There it is!" he yelled as he shook hands with Justin. "Welcome to the family, Justin!"

Justin laughed awkwardly along with him.

At the counter, Alex took a seat on one of the stools while her mom cleaned up, and her dad and Justin talked sports.

"Justin is a great catch," her mom said, watching him chat with her husband. She leaned in closer to Alex. "You should go out with him."

"Ew, gross," Alex said, wrinkling her nose.

"That's exactly how I felt about your father when I first met him," her mom confessed. Then she gazed at her husband and sighed. "And now he's my big cuddly bug."

Now Alex felt like she was going to be sick! "Ew, grosser!" she exclaimed.

Her dad walked up behind her. "Justin is a fine young man," he said. "You should be more like him."

What?! Alex couldn't believe it! She was still being compared to Justin. She got off her seat and walked over to her brother. "Even when they don't know you, they want me to be more like you!" she complained.

Justin shrugged. "You can't wish away quality," he said.

Alex sighed. This situation had gone from bad to worse. What was she going to do now?

Chapter Six

In the Russos' living room later that night, Justin and Alex were both in their pajamas. Justin had made up a bed on the sofa, but he couldn't go to sleep without a plan in place first. "Okay, how are you going to get the genie back?" he asked Alex.

Alex paced around the room. "I don't know," she said honestly. "I've been racking my brain. I just wish the genie would show up."

Suddenly, there was a *poof*! and the genie appeared. "Whoa!" the genie exclaimed.

"What just happened?" Alex asked Justin in disbelief.

"You *wished* for the genie to come back, and she came back," Justin told her.

The genie walked over to Alex. "And stumbling on that," she said, "you just used your second wish."

The scoreboard magically dropped, and a big *X* appeared under the second wish.

"Okay Alex, you have one wish left," Justin advised. "Choose your words *really* carefully."

"I know, I know!" Alex said, feeling flustered. "I wish you would just stop telling me—" she stopped in midsentence. She had almost used her third wish! Pacing around in circles, she started to think out loud. "Ah!" she said, then shook her head. "That's not it! That's not it. I'm going to get this right. Okay. I wish people would—no, no, no." She continued to pace. "Uh, I wish Justin would be—no, no, no. You'll wreck that. I wish . . . My first wish . . . I wish my brother . . ."

The genie plopped down on a chair and laughed. "Ooh, this is going to be good."

"Oh! I've got it!" Alex exclaimed. Her face lit up with a broad smile.

Justin moved closer to Alex. "Uh, hold up," he said. "Let me hear it."

But Alex went ahead and blurted out her third wish. "Okay, I wish everyone would see Justin clearly for who he is."

"Wait," Justin tried to stop her. "There could be a problem if you say the word . . . clearly!"

But Justin was too late. As soon as Alex spoke those words, Justin disappeared! Alex looked around. All she could see was a pair of pajamas floating in midair. Justin was invisible!

The scoreboard appeared again, and this time, all three X's were marked.

"And that's my triple play," the genie said

smugly. She opened the door to leave. "Thanks for rubbing my lamp. Really. It's yours to keep. In fact, use it as a gravy boat. Just remember, it's not dishwasher safe. You know what?" she said, changing her mind. "Throw it in the dishwasher—I don't even care." And then she walked out the door.

"Alex, look what you've done!" the invisible Justin cried. "You ruined my life!"

"Hold on," Alex said. "You're *invisible*. Isn't there something you've always wanted to do? Someone you've always wanted to get back at and they would never know because you're invisible?"

Suddenly, something bopped Alex on the head.

"There," Justin said. "I've done it."

Alex gave in. "Okay, I had that coming."

"Now fix this!" Justin pleaded.

"Hey, you kids want some ice cream?" Mr. Russo called from upstairs.

In a panic, Alex looked over in the direction of the invisible Justin. His pajamas suddenly fell to the floor. "What are you doing?" she asked in horror.

"This way I'll be totally invisible," he explained.

Alex made a face. "Ew! No, just hide!" She pointed toward the kitchen.

Mr. Russo came down the stairs. "Where's your friend?" he asked, looking around.

"Bathroom?" Alex said, trying to sound casual.

"Oh," Mr. Russo said. Taking the opportunity to tell Alex how much he liked Justin, he continued, "I love talking sports with him. I'll just sit right here and wait until he gets back."

As he went to sit down on one of the chairs, Alex realized that Justin was already sitting there! She rushed to her dad to stop him. "No, no, not there!" she shouted.

"Why not?" her father asked, confused.

"Because I'm going to sit there," Alex said quickly. "I like sitting there."

"Get off!" an invisible Justin yelped.

"Hey! Oh!" Mr. Russo said, looking around. "Who was that?"

"Uh . . ." Alex said, with a guilty look on her face.

"Alex Russo," her dad said, "what is going on here . . . and why is there a pillow floating in midair?" he asked sternly, pointing in the pillow's direction.

Alex knew that was the last straw. She had to tell the truth. But it sounded so unbelievable! "Justin's invisible!" she spat out.

Mrs. Russo suddenly rushed into the room. "Jerry, what's wrong?" she asked.

Mr. Russo looked at his wife, shaking his head. "I just sat down on Alex's invisible friend, Justin."

Not knowing where to look, Mrs. Russo called, "Justin, what did Alex do to you?"

"Yeah, I don't know," Mr. Russo said, trying to remain calm. An outsider couldn't know that the Russo family used magic! "And I'm sure this may *seem* like magic, but I'm sure there's a perfectly rational, scientific explanation for all of it—"

Alex interrupted him. "Dad, Justin knows about magic," she said.

Mr. Russo relaxed. "Okay, what did she do to you?" he asked the invisible Justin.

The green pillow began to float in the air again. "Well, she—" Justin began to say.

"Wait," Mrs. Russo cried. "Is he holding that pillow to—" She stopped herself, realizing that even though he was invisible, Justin was using the pillow to cover himself up. Quickly, Justin grabbed the sculpture that Harper had made. "Uh, just talk to Uncle Ernesto," he said, holding it up to where his face would have been. The sculpture floated in midair as the invisible Justin held it.

Mrs. Russo turned to her daughter. "Alex, what did you do to him?" she demanded.

Alex sat down and took a deep breath. "Okay, I'll tell you," she said. "But you're never going to believe me."

"Of course we'll believe you!" Mr. Russo exclaimed.

"Justin is my brother. And your oldest son," Alex told her parents.

"I don't believe you," her father replied immediately.

"No, it's true!" Alex protested. "I made a wish with the genie that everyone would stop comparing me to Justin, but the genie conned me and made everyone forget him, and then he became invisible!"

Just then, a voice from behind the sculpture spoke. "She's telling the truth!"

Still not convinced, Mrs. Russo folded her arms. "You're trying to tell me I have a son I don't even *remember*?" she asked.

Alex jumped up. "Please, believe me. You have to believe me," she pleaded. "I used up all my wishes, but the genie was too smart for me."

Mr. Russo suddenly understood. He turned to his wife to explain. "Genies *are* sneaky," he pointed out.

Alex looked at her parents pleadingly. "You have to help me. You can't let him be invisible forever." She was feeling pretty bad about the situation. "I grew up with him. He may be dorky and annoying, but he's fun and gullible enough to pull pranks on, and he's my brother. I need him back!"

Mrs. Russo put her arm around her daughter's shoulders. "You know what, honey?" she said. "I think I believe you. You really love your brother."

"You love him, too," Alex said softly to her mother.

"And sometimes more than her," Justin,

referring to his sister, added from somewhere in the room.

"I'm trying to help you here," Alex said through gritted teeth. She exhaled deeply and then continued. "We have to do something."

Her dad walked over to her. "Uh, honey, I believe you, too," he said, giving her a squeeze. "But what am I going to do? The genie outsmarted you."

This was not what Alex had expected to hear. What could she do now? "Justin, I'm sorry," she said sincerely.

Always looking on the bright side, Mrs. Russo piped up. "But I'm happy I have another son." She laughed and held out her arms. "Let me have a hug." But then she stopped herself. "Well, go put some clothes on first."

Justin agreed. "I'll be right back," he said.

Everyone watched as the green pillow sailed out of the room. Max, who had been woken up by all the commotion, came into the room just as the pillow was floating out.

"Aha!" he exclaimed. "Floating pillow. You've got to teach me that one so I can sleep standing up."

Suddenly, Alex had an idea. "You know what?" she said to her parents. "The genie may have outsmarted me, but maybe we can out-dumb *her*." She turned to face her younger brother. "Max, how would you get a genie to come back to her lamp?"

"I know!" Max said full of confidence. "Orange soda."

"What?" Alex said.

Max nodded his head. "If someone poured orange soda in my room," he told them. "I'd be really mad."

"You spilled orange soda in your room, didn't you?" his mother said knowingly. "What did we say about taking that up there?" She left in a huff to go check out the mess.

"See?" Max gloated. "She's really mad and she's going to my room."

Alex smiled. Leave it to Max to come up with a scheme to out-dumb a genie! Now she only hoped that the plan would work. Justin's future depended on it!

Chapter Seven

Alex and Max huddled together in the kitchen as they watched their dad carefully pour orange soda into the genie's lamp.

"Is it working? Is it working?" Alex asked impatiently. She craned her neck to see around her father. There was no sign of the genie anywhere. Frustrated, Alex reached out and grabbed the genie's lamp. "It's not working!" Alex yelled, frantically shaking the lamp.

But just at that moment, the genie appeared. She was *not* happy!

"What are you doing?" she growled. "That's my house!"

"See?" Max said. He puffed out his chest proudly. "Nothing drives the ladies mad like orange soda."

"I'll stop shaking it if you give Max a wish," Alex told her, holding the lamp, which was filled with fizzing soda. "It's just going to get foamier in here."

Alarmed, the genie gave in. "Fine," she said. "What do you want?"

"I wish for this haircut and a shirt like this," Max said, and pointed to himself, trying to be clever.

"I can't give you a wish for something you already have!" the genie responded. Then she paused, and narrowed her eyes. "What game are you playing, kid?"

"I wish for the genie game," Max told her.

"*What* genie game? What are you trying to do?" the genie asked.

Max stepped toward her. "Oh, you know what I'm trying to do," he said.

The genie looked around nervously. Max had backed her into a corner. "Well, it sounds like you're trying to find out about the reset button," she said. As soon as she spoke those words, the genie's hand flew to her mouth.

Alex clapped and grinned with excitement. "Max, there's a reset button!" Now all her brother had to do was make a wish that would reverse this whole mess! Giving him an encouraging smile, she nodded. "You know what to wish for."

"Swimming pool of pudding?" he asked, his eyes wide with excitement. "Yes!"

"No," Alex said, sighing. "The reset button."

Though he was disappointed that he wouldn't get his wish, Max did as he was told.

"I wish you would show me the reset button," he said.

"In your lamp!" Alex added.

"In your lamp," Max repeated.

"If there's a reset button," Mr. Russo said, already scheming, "we'll need this paper clip." Then he saw the genie looking straight at him. "Hi," he said meekly.

Suddenly, a swirl of magic swept the Russos and the genie into the lamp!

"Whoa!" Mr. Russo cried, trying to keep his head above the fizz.

The bubbles were everywhere! "Ooh, orangey," Alex said, licking her lips.

Mr. Russo looked around in a panic. "Max!" he yelled.

"I got it!" Max cried as he jumped out of the bubbles. Because they had become smaller to fit inside the lamp, the paper clip Mr. Russo had brought with them was huge! Max could barely hold on to it.

"Go!" Alex urged him.

Reluctantly, the genie showed them the reset button on the wall. "All right. Here it is," she said. "When you press it, it undoes all the things you've wished for as if they'd never happened."

As soon as the paper clip was inserted into the button, the scoreboard dropped and the three X's on it disappeared. The Russos' plan had worked!

In an instant, Alex, Max, and Mr. Russo were back in their living room with Mrs. Russo. After Alex had caught her breath, she looked around and spotted Justin!

"Phew," Justin said, happy to see that his body was visible again. "That was close."

"Oh!" Mrs. Russo exclaimed when she saw Justin. She reached out and gave him a hug.

"You're back!" Alex cheered. "I'm so glad I can see you."

"Oh, Justin, sweetie," Mrs. Russo gushed. "I'm so sorry I forgot you."

Mr. Russo walked over to his wife. "What kind of mother forgets her own son?" he teased.

"What about you?" she asked, teasing him back.

"What?" Mr. Russo said innocently. "I'm a dad. Before my cup of coffee, I'm lucky if I remember *one* of these kids." He turned to Max. "Come on. Bedtime."

Max headed up to his room with his parents. Once Justin and Alex were alone, Justin looked over at his sister.

"So, you were pretty upset about me being invisible, huh?" he asked.

Alex stood up, trying to avoid the conversation. She had forgotten that Justin was in the room when she had said all that mushy stuff about him. Alexis went over to the couch that was still made up as a bed. "No, I was just afraid that I would be running into you all the time," she scoffed.

"No you weren't," he said. Justin put on his best sad face and began to whine, pretending to be Alex. "I need my brother back. I need my brother back. Where is he?"

"Yeah, I'm glad you're back," Alex said sweetly. "That way, I can do this!" She turned quickly, grabbed a pillow, and bopped it over Justin's head.

Justin kept up the act, crying out, "I miss my brother! He's so—"

Alex hit him on the head with the pillow again. She certainly didn't bring him back so he could make fun of her. But truth be told, she *was* really happy to have him home. She might get hard quiz questions because of him, she might get in trouble because of him, and she might get recruited by the math team because of him, but Justin was her big brother. And Alex didn't want to change that fact at all.

PART
TWO

Chapter One

Regular school had just ended for the day, and Justin, Alex, and Max were in the Wizard's Lair for their magic lessons with their dad. Justin was giving an oral report—and boring everyone! Alex and Max had fallen asleep sitting up, and Mr. Russo was fighting to keep his eyes open.

"And that's when the great Chinese wizard Li first used dragon scales to build an impenetrable box for safeguarding one's wand," Justin said, not noticing that no one was paying attention. "And then, in the twelfth century, there were nine native—"

But then Mr. Russo glanced at his watch and held up his hand. "Time!" he exclaimed. "You're supposed to keep your oral reports under forty-five minutes. Otherwise you start losing people. Okay, Alex, you're up."

But Alex was in a deep sleep, thanks to Justin's extremely long speech.

"Alex!" her dad shouted.

Jumping up, Alex looked around in a panic. Her movement woke up Max, too, and he bumped his head on the wall behind him.

"Uh-huh?" Alex said. Then she realized where she was and quickly rebounded. "Oh, yeah," she said, pretending to know what was going on in the lesson.

"Your report on crystal balls: history, usage, and manufacturing," her dad said, trying to remain patient.

"I got a hard quiz question because of Justin!"
Alex complained.

Alex reached out and grabbed the genie lamp. "So, are
we going to take this genie out or what?" she asked.

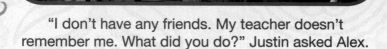

"I don't have any friends. My teacher doesn't remember me. What did you do?" Justin asked Alex.

"Hey, who's your new friend?" Mrs. Russo asked Alex when she saw Justin.

Alex made her third wish: "Okay, I wish everyone would see Justin clearly for who he is."

"Alex, what did you do to Justin?"
Mrs. Russo demanded.

Mr. Russo, Alex, and Max huddled together as Alex poured orange soda into the genie lamp.

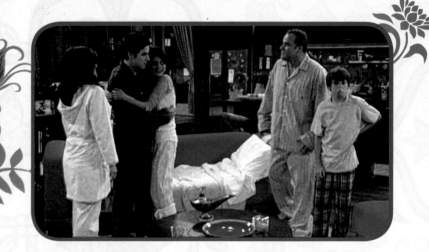

"You're back!" Alex cheered, giving Justin a hug.

PART TWO

The Russos were totally exhausted while Justin gave a very long report.

"What are the answers to my social studies test?" Max asked the leprechaun answer-blower.

"The kids are out having fun with their uncle. It's a good thing," Mrs. Russo told Mr. Russo.

"Who is my secret admirer?" Justin asked.

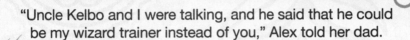

"Uncle Kelbo and I were talking, and he said that he could be my wizard trainer instead of you," Alex told her dad.

"The lunch lady loves you," Max told Justin.

"You're going to teach me about time travel?"
Alex asked her uncle hopefully.

A spell gone wrong turned Alex into a sea creature!

Justin laughed, patting his brother on the back. Now that the mystery of the love letters was solved, he felt pretty good. And he really *was* honored that the lunch lady had picked him!

In a different hallway at school, Alex walked out of her class and spotted the lunch lady waiting for her. "Hey, thanks for doing that for me, Doris," she called. "Here's the left-handed mashed-potato scooper you wanted." Alex handed the serving utensil to her.

"Thanks," Doris said, beaming. "A lot of people think it's the same as an ice-cream scooper. Those people would be wrong."

As Alex walked away, she couldn't help but grin. "That was totally an ice-cream scooper," she mumbled to herself. But it was worth every penny to get Justin to believe that all those pink love letters were coming from the *lunch lady*! It was the perfect prank!

Chapter Six

In the lair later that day, Mr. Russo was coming to the end of his lecture. "So *that's* how you disappear and reappear ten feet away," he said. He cracked a smile. "Pretty fun, huh?"

"That's about as magical as walking," Justin said, rolling his eyes. He was really bored.

Suddenly, the door lit up and Alex and Uncle Kelbo walked into the room. "See? What did I tell you? Not as much fun as *poofing* in," she complained to her uncle. She turned to her dad. "Hey, Dad."

"Hey, Alex," her dad said. "You missed a good one today. We disappeared and then reappeared ten feet away." He looked to his sons for support. "Wasn't it fun, guys?"

"Yeah, a little more exciting than that ripening fruit spell you taught us," Justin said sarcastically.

"Okay," Mr. Russo said, not quite getting his son's joke. "Well, have a good lesson. The lair is yours, Kelbo. Please leave it how you found it. Come on, guys." He motioned for the boys to follow. "Ooh! Hey, Max," Mr. Russo called before they left the room. "Uh, does anybody want some salted nuts?" He presented a can for Max to open.

"Sure, Dad," Max said flatly. This was the oldest—and most boring—prank ever. Max opened the can, and out popped the usual snakes on springs.

"Wow! Snakes of all different colors!" Mr. Russo cried. He looked around the room to see everyone's reaction, but he was met with blank stares. Defeated, he quickly followed his sons out of the room. Maybe it wasn't his best prank, but the kids used to love it!

Once her dad and two brothers were gone, Alex flopped down onto the sofa. "So what's our lesson going to be?" she asked her uncle.

Kelbo stretched and let out a loud yawn. "I thought we'd take a nap first . . ." He started to doze off but sat up when he saw Alex's concerned face. "Well, I'll tell you what it's *not* going to be, and that's fruit ripening," he told her. "Because it's easy! All you do is: you buy the fruit, you go into the future, fruit's ripe, you eat it!"

Alex straightened up. "You're going to teach me about time travel?" she asked hopefully. "I've always wanted to learn that!"

But before Kelbo could answer, a letter

magically shot through the door. "Oh, look!" Kelbo yelled, happy for a distraction. He got up and walked over to the letter. "The wizard mail's here!"

"Uncle Kelbo," Alex protested, "can we please focus on the lesson?" She watched as he picked up the mail.

"Look," he explained, holding the letter, "we'll read it. We'll go back in time to before we read it, and it'll be like we haven't even read it."

Alex was unsure. She checked the envelope and instantly grew disappointed. "A sca-chimp sample? We used to get these all the time when we were little. They're just pets you put in water, and you don't even have to feed them or play with them."

Kelbo disagreed. "They're great," he said. "Open them up. Come on!"

Alex looked at the envelope again. She was still skeptical. "I don't know," she said cautiously. "These aren't regular sea chimps. They came in the wizard mail, and Dad doesn't like us to open the wizard mail without him, because some of the stuff can be dangerous."

Kelbo was getting impatient. "Okay, I understand," he said, trying to sway Alex with his logic. "But your dad's not your teacher. I am. And whatever goes wrong, we can fix with magic."

How could Alex argue that? "All right," she agreed. "But don't you need water for sea chimps?"

Just as she said that, Kelbo ripped open the envelope and a stream of water came rushing out.

"Apparently not," Alex said, correcting herself.

Kelbo grabbed a mug, held it under the stream, and took a big gulp. But the water still kept pouring out!

"That's not going to work!" Alex screamed. The water was gushing now! "Fix it with magic!" she yelled, panicked.

"Hmm. Okay, okay, okay," Kelbo said, pretending to know the solution. "All right. I got it!"

Alex looked at her uncle nervously. The water was rushing out of the envelope faster now. At this rate, the room would be completely underwater in minutes!

Suddenly, her uncle looked extremely worried. "I can't!" Kelbo yelled. "I'm panicking!"

Alex was panicking, too! How could her uncle not know how to fix this? Her dad was going to kill her—if she didn't drown first!

Chapter Seven

Back at the Waverly Sub Station, Max saw Justin sitting at one of the tables. He quickly slipped a hairnet over his head and paraded over to his older brother. "Guess who I am?" Max cleared his throat and tried to speak in a high-pitched voice. "I'm the lunch lady. I'm in love with Justin. Give me a kiss, doll face."

Justin backed away from Max's puckered lips.

Max laughed until he looked up to see a man storming into the restaurant. "Hey, why is Coach Gunderson here? And why does he look so mad?" Max asked.

Huffing over to Justin's table, the coach looked at the two Russo boys. "Which one of you is Justin Russo?" he demanded.

Max and Justin immediately pointed at each other. Justin knew Coach Gunderson had a reputation—and it wasn't for being sweet!

"I think it's *you*," the coach said to Justin, pointing his large finger right in Justin's face. "You don't shower after gym. Because you don't *sweat*. Because you *walk* the mile."

"Hey, Coach," Justin said soothingly, trying to calm him down.

"What are you doing writing love letters to my girlfriend, the lunch lady?" the coach interrupted.

"Uh . . ." Justin stuttered. "She was putting letters in my locker, and I was just trying to let her down gently."

From across the restaurant, Mrs. Russo saw the commotion and walked over to the table. "Uh, excuse me," she said. "What's going on here?"

"Your son is trying to tell me that he's getting love letters from my girlfriend, the lunch lady!" the coach spat out.

Now it was Mrs. Russo's turn to be shocked. "The *lunch* lady?" she asked in surprise. "May I see one of those notes?"

"I have one," Max said, pulling a pink scrap of paper from his pocket. He handed the letter to his mom, and Justin glared at him. Max tore off for the kitchen, figuring he had done enough damage for one day.

Mrs. Russo read the letter out loud: "I love your light-saber night-light," she said, and immediately stopped reading. She looked up at Justin. "How would the lunch lady know you have a light-saber night-light?"

Then Justin knew exactly how the *lunch lady* would know about his night-light. "Alex," he said, seething.

Mrs. Russo understood, too. "Alex is my fourteen-year-old daughter, and she kind of torments him," Mrs. Russo explained to the coach.

"I get it," the coach said. His expression softened. "You still sleep with a night-light?" he asked Justin. When Justin nodded, he continued on. "Good. The dark can be very, very scary. Keep walking the mile. And, uh, sorry I barked at you. Lunch lady says I get pretty jealous." He laughed, a little embarrassed, and then rushed out of the restaurant.

Mrs. Russo and Justin watched Coach Gunderson leave. Then, suddenly, they heard a scream from the kitchen.

"Dad!" Justin cried, as he and his mom

entered the kitchen. Mr. Russo was sprawled out on the floor on his back.

"Honey, are you all right?" Mrs. Russo said, racing toward him.

"Uh, yeah," Mr. Russo said shakily, as he slowly stood up. The pie that he had been carrying on a serving tray was now all over his face. "I don't know what happened," he said, wiping whipped cream from his forehead.

"*I* know what happened," Max said. He pointed to the door of the lair. "There's water coming out of the lair." They all turned to look.

"Oh, who—who's in the lair?" Mrs. Russo asked, a concerned look on her face.

Justin walked over to the door. "Alex and Kelbo," he told her. "They're doing their lesson in there."

"Okay," Mr. Russo said, trying to remain calm. "Somebody's got to get into the lair."

But Mrs. Russo was not so calm. "We don't

know how much water is in there. If we open it, it could flood the whole restaurant!"

Justin gasped. This was serious! He looked at his dad.

Mr. Russo considered the potentially disastrous situation. He had to act quickly—and wisely. Suddenly, he had an idea. "Hey, you remember that spell from today?" he said to Justin. "Transporting ten feet? Come on!"

"I'm on it!" Justin yelled.

"Whoa!" his dad called out. "Wait, wait! I'll be right back!" He raced out of the kitchen and quickly returned, wearing a wet suit appropriate for deep-sea diving. "Okay, okay. I'm ready. Better safe than sorry," he said, noticing his wife's raised eyebrows. "Justin, get me in there."

Justin took a deep breath. He couldn't risk messing this up! "*Threemetrus-movetrus!*" he chanted—and hoped that the spell would work.

Chapter Eight

Inside the lair, two sea chimps were floating in the water.

"Hey, why can I breathe underwater?" Alex wondered out loud as she swam around.

"Uh, it's due to the fact that we're sea chimps," Kelbo explained.

"Do something!" she cried. She hadn't exactly planned on turning into a sea chimp who floated around with curly antennae and a mermaid's tail!

"Relax," Kelbo said, coaxing her. "I've been in way worse situations than this. Imagine the exact same thing, except hot lava."

"Why were you in hot lava?" Alex asked, intrigued.

"Suffice it to say," Kelbo replied, "I don't know how to make hot coffee."

At that moment, Alex saw her dad float into the room in full scuba gear.

"You opened a magic sea-chimp package, didn't you?" her dad asked through his diving mask as soon as he spotted her.

"A little," she confessed.

Mr. Russo was *not* pleased, but he knew he had to get everyone out of this situation before he could think about anything else. "I know a spell that'll fix this. Alex, repeat after me: 'I'm a big knucklehead,'" he said.

Alex did as she was told. "I'm a big knucklehead," she repeated. Then she realized what she had just said. "Wait a second. That's not a spell."

Her dad grinned. "No, I know. I just wanted to hear you admit it."

Floating closer to his brother, Kelbo swished his large, green, sea-chimp tail. "Hey, if anyone here's a big knucklehead," he joked, "it's this sea chimp!"

"Gee, who knows a spell that'll get us out of this mess? Anyone?" Mr. Russo asked, glaring at his brother. "Oh, wait, I do!" he said, answering his own question. He swam over to Alex. "All right, Alex! Say this: *dehydratus-lougaines, apus-escapus.*"

Alex did as she was told. "*Dehydratus-lougaines, apus-escapus,*" she repeated.

Instantly, the water disappeared. Mr. Russo could always be counted on to come to the rescue!

Back in the Russos living room with her parents, brothers, and uncle, Alex dried off with a towel. "I just don't get it. Kelbo said he could fix it, but he couldn't . . . and Dad could," she said, looking at her father and uncle. Kelbo had a towel wrapped around his head. Then she looked at her brothers in disbelief. "But Dad's not even a wizard anymore," she said, confused.

"Well, your dad was always a much better wizard than I was," Kelbo admitted.

"That can't be true," Justin told him. "Only one wizard in each family can keep their powers. If Dad was the better wizard, he'd have kept his powers."

Kelbo turned to Mr. Russo, shocked. "You never told them, huh?" he asked his brother.

Alex stepped forward. What were they hiding? "Told us what?"

"Honey, I think they're old enough," Mrs. Russo said, coming to her husband's side.

Jumping up from his seat, Max cried, "We're all getting go-carts?"

"No," his dad told him, shaking his head.

Mrs. Russo moved closer to her children. "When Kelbo and your father competed to see who'd keep their wizard powers," she told her kids, "it was your dad who won the contest."

"What?" Alex exclaimed. She couldn't believe no one had ever told her that story. She thought her dad had *lost* his family wizard competition.

Her mother continued on. "But wizards can't marry nonwizards," she said. She touched her husband's shoulder lovingly. "So your dad gave Kelbo his powers so that he could marry me."

Alex walked over to her parents, smiling. "I think that's the sweetest thing I've ever heard in my life," she gushed.

"Give your powers up for a girl?" Max asked incredulously. "What?"

"Yeah, right!" Justin agreed. That was ridiculous!

"You guys," Alex explained to her brothers.

"If Dad hadn't given up his powers, none of us would be here."

Mr. Russo nodded his head. "Yeah. I made the right decision then, and I stand by it." He gave his wife a big hug.

"And I should've stood by you, Dad," Alex told him, fully realizing the mistake she had made. "Will you still be my wizard teacher?"

Kelbo leaped forward. "Please! I beg of you, okay?" he pleaded to Mr. Russo. "Take her on. You know me. I can't handle it. I—I get distracted, and then I get careless, and then . . ." his hands flew up to his head where he felt the fluffy towel. "Oh, this towel is so soft. Oh, and distracted!" he said, realizing that he was getting sidetracked. "You know, I get distracted!"

"We get it," Mr. Russo told him. He looked at Alex. "Honey, I'll be your teacher." He gently put his hand on her shoulder.

Alex smiled at her dad. Then she turned to

her uncle. "But you're still my fun Uncle Kelbo," she told him. "I mean, who else gets to say that they were a sea chimp, even for a little while?"

"Actually, everyone I know," Kelbo admitted. He laughed. "I've made them all open up that same packet because I just love the pretty colors on the outside."

Mr. Russo looked down at his watch. "Whoa. The basketball game is on!"

"Oh, can I watch it with you?" Alex asked, eager to spend some time with her dad.

Her dad smiled. "Yes. I'd love that, honey."

"Wait, wait, wait!" Kelbo exclaimed. "I've got an idea. We can all watch it!"

Before anyone could say anything, Kelbo recited a spell that transported the whole family to the wizard box at the basketball game.

"Hey, guys, want to see something cool?" Alex asked when they were settled in their seats. "Hold your heads like this." She showed them how to put their hands above their ears and hold on.

Max, who wasn't paying attention, missed the instructions. "Oh, what are you talking about?" he asked. But no one heard him.

"*Cranium revolvus*!" Alex yelled.

Not having heard the directions, Max's head twirled all the way around, along with the heads of the other wizards in the box. He was not a happy camper! But the rest of the Russos broke out into giggles.

As Alex laughed along with her family, she realized how much she liked spending time with them. Even though being Justin's little sister was sometimes hard, and even though her dad was sometimes strict, she wouldn't have traded being a Russo for anything!

Something magical is on the way!
Look for the next book in Disney's
Wizards of Waverly Place series.

Super Switch!

Adapted by Heather Alexander

Based on the series created by Todd J. Greenwald

Part One is based on the episode "Disenchanted Evening," Written by Jack Sanderson

Part Two is based on the episode "Report Card," Written by Gigi McCreery & Perry Rein & Peter Murrieta

Alex Russo slowly pulled a brush through her long, wavy brown hair. She gazed at her reflection in the bathroom mirror and then glanced at the clock. Yikes! Late as usual.

Alex grabbed a sparkly clip and snapped it in her hair. She raced out of the apartment and down the spiral staircase that led to her family's restaurant in New York's Greenwich Village, the Waverly Sub Station. As she rushed down the stairs, her two brothers, Justin and Max, were right in front of her. They were running late, too.

Mrs. Russo handed Alex's older brother, Justin, his brown-bag lunch. "Okay. Whole wheat," she said. "No crust." Mrs. Russo passed a second brown bag to Max, the youngest Russo sibling. She deposited the last paper bag in Alex's hand.

Alex sighed. She really wasn't into sandwiches. Maybe it was because her family owned a sandwich shop and she had to make and serve sandwiches after school every day.

"Oh," Mrs. Russo said, noticing Alex's short-sleeved shirt, "you might want to put on a jacket because it's very chilly outside."

Alex rolled her eyes. Her mother could be *so* annoying sometimes! The weather was fine.

But she knew her mom would insist. "Fine. Stop all the racket, I'll wear a jacket." She smiled at her rhyme. Then she snapped her fingers, and a cute white jean jacket magically appeared over her shoulders.

"Hey!" Mr. Russo hurried out from behind the sandwich-shop counter.

"Hey!" Alex greeted her dad.

"No, not 'hey.' I meant '*Hey!*'" He sounded annoyed. "When your mom said to put on a jacket, she meant go get one, not pop one on."

"What's the big deal? It's just a jacket." Alex didn't know why her dad was so irritated. It wasn't as if he didn't know she was a wizard. So were Justin and Max. And Mr. Russo used to be a one, too. They were a family of wizards. At the age of eighteen, only one of the Russo kids would actually be able to keep their magical powers, but until then, they would try to learn as much magic as possible. Of course, no one was ever supposed to find out that they were wizards. But the restaurant was empty. So what was the problem with a little fun? Alex wondered.

"The big deal is, today it's just a jacket. But how long is it going to be before you're popping a calculator into a math test?" her mom demanded.

"First it's cheating on math, then it's cheating on everything," her dad said sternly. "Then this happens, then that happens . . . then you're in jail," he concluded, his face grim.

"This happens and *that* happens?" Alex was incredulous. Her parents could be so dramatic! "I just didn't want to walk upstairs."

"Well, walk upstairs, take that jacket off, then come back down and put it back on," her dad instructed.

Alex sighed. There'd be no winning this one. She trudged back up the stairs. "Anything to keep me out of jail," she muttered, walking out.

"Hey, Maxy, what's in the box?" Mrs. Russo asked her son. She walked over to a table and inspected a plain shoe box that was sitting next to Max's backpack.

"Oh, it's my Mars diorama for school," he said proudly.

Mrs. Russo reached into the box and scooped up a handful of sand. "Where's the Mars part?" she asked. She laughed as the sand fell through her fingers. "It's just a bunch of beach sand."

"Well, it's a pretty"—Max pulled out the teacher's instruction sheet and quickly read it over—"barren planet."

"What does 'barren' mean?" Justin challenged. Justin loved words. In fact, he loved anything to do with school. Of course, it was easy to love your school when you were one of the smartest kids in it!

Max glanced at his project. "Sandy?" he said hopefully.

His mother sighed. "We'll discuss this later. You need to work harder, young man."

"Come on." Justin grabbed his little brother's diorama. "Let's get your sandbox to school before a cat finds it."

Max groaned as he followed Justin out the door. Last night, he'd thought he'd done a decent job. Now he realized his Mars shoe box looked like a litter box. He sure hoped his teacher had a good imagination!

Alex bounded down the stairs for the second time that morning. "You see? Now I'm late." She pointed to the clock. "Can you at least write me a note?" she asked her dad.

"Sure," Mr. Russo agreed reluctantly. He pulled out his order pad and a pencil.

"Okay." Alex thought for a second, then began to dictate. "Dear Principal, Alex is late because her dad is a meanie for not letting her use magic to zap a jacket on." She looked up at her dad. He wasn't smiling. Or writing. "Okay,

I'll run to school," Alex decided. She grabbed her messenger bag and dashed out the door.

She was barely down the block when she spotted a classmate of hers across the street, carrying a huge binder.

"Hey, there's T. J.," she said aloud to herself. At that moment, T. J. tripped on a crack in the sidewalk. He pitched forward and the binder flew from his arms. Alex started to cover her eyes so she wouldn't have to watch, but then time seemed to freeze. T. J. hovered midfall, both he and his binder floating in the air. Alex gasped as the binder turned and flew back into T. J.'s arms and he magically stood back up. He glanced about nervously then—*poof*!— he disappeared!

"Hey. Are you a—you just—wha—" Alex was so amazed that she couldn't form words. Did she really just see what she thought she'd seen? Definitely, she decided. "Look, wizard!" she managed to cry.

She had just found another teenage wizard—and he went to her school! Wow, Alex thought. What are the odds of that? Whatever the case, I'm definitely going to find out more about T. J.!